CLEVER CAKES

MICHAEL ROSEN

WITH ILLUSTRATIONS BY
ASHLEY KING

Barrington Stoke

First published in 2020 in Great Britain by
Barrington Stoke Ltd
18 Walker Street, Edinburgh, EH3 7LP

www.barringtonstoke.co.uk

Text © 2020 Michael Rosen
Illustrations © 2020 Ashley King

First published in a collection, *Clever Cakes* (Walker, 1991)

A CIP catalogue record for this book is available
from the British Library upon request

ISBN: 978-1-78112-928-9

CONTENTS

CLEVER CAKES

Once there was a girl called Masha, who lived with her granny at the edge of the woods.

One day Masha said, "Granny, can I play outside with my friends?"

"Yes, Masha," said Granny, "but don't run off into the woods, will you? There are big bad animals there that bite ..."

Off went Masha to play with her friends. They played hide-and-seek.

Masha went away to hide and she hid right deep in the woods. Then she waited for her friends to find her.

She waited and waited but they never came.

So Masha came out of her hiding place and started to walk home.

She went this way, then that way, but very soon she knew she was lost.

"He-e-e-lp!" she shouted. "He-e-e-elp!"

But no one came.

Then very suddenly up came a massive muscly bear.

"Ah hah!" said the bear. "You come with me, little girl. I'm taking you home. I want you to cook my dinner, wash my trousers and scrub the floor in my house."

"I don't want to do that or anything like it, thank you very much," said Masha. "I want to go home."

"Oh no you don't," said the bear. "You're coming home with me."

And he picked up Masha in his massive muscly paws and took her off to his house.

So now Masha had to cook and clean and wash and dust all day long. And she hated it. And she hated the massive muscly bear. So she made a plan.

She cooked some cakes and then she said to the bear, "Mr Bear, please can I take some cakes to my granny?"

I'm not falling for a stupid trick like that, thought the bear. *If I let her go to her granny's, she'll never come back.*

"No, you can't," he said. "I'll take your cakes to her myself."

And he thought, *I'll eat all those cakes. Yum, yum and yum again.*

"Right," said Masha, "I'll put these cakes in this basket. Don't eat them on the way to Granny's, will you? Cos if you do, something terrible will happen to you."

"Of course I won't eat the cakes," said the bear.

As soon as the bear wasn't looking, Masha jumped into the basket.

Then the bear picked up the basket and walked off.

After a while, the bear got tired – ooh, that basket was so heavy, it was pulling off his arm – so he sat down.

"Now for the cakes," he said.

But Masha called out from inside
the basket, "Don't you eat us, Mr Bear.
We're little cakes for Masha's granny."

You should have seen that bear jump!

"The cakes heard me!" he said.
"Oh, yes, Masha did say if I ate them
something terrible would happen to me.
I'd better leave them alone."

So up got the bear and walked on …
and on … and on … until he began to feel
hungry.

He thought, *If I could eat the cakes without them knowing, then perhaps nothing terrible will happen to me. But how can I eat them without them knowing?* Then he said out loud, "Oooh, I wonder if those little cakes would like to hop out of the basket and come for a walk with me."

But Masha called out from inside the basket, "Don't you dare touch us, you great greedy glut. We're little cakes for Masha's granny."

The bear nearly jumped out of his jacket.

"Woo hoo, those clever little cakes knew that was a trick. Next time I won't say anything at all. I'll just sit down and gobble them up. Yum, yum and yum again."

So up he got and walked on ... and on ... and on ...

But now the bear was getting really very, very hungry. It felt like there was an enormous hole in his belly.

This time he remembered not to say a word. He sat down slo-o-o-o-wly and slo-o-o-o-wly he put out his massive muscly paw to pick up a cake.

But Masha was peeking through the holes in the basket and she saw what the bear was up to, so she called out, "Don't you dare touch us, you horrible great greedy glut! We're little cakes for Masha's granny and if you touch us, we'll jump out of the basket faster than you can blink and we'll eat you up, ears and all."

"Zoo-wow, those cakes must be magic!" said the bear. "I'd be crazy to touch them. I'd better take them to Masha's granny as quickly as I can or something terrible will happen to me." And he hurried on to Granny's house.

When he got there, he shouted, "Open the door, Granny!"

Granny came to the door and when she saw a great big bear standing there she was scared stiff.

But little Masha called out from the basket, "Look out, Mr Bear, your time's up. Now we're going to eat you."

The bear dropped the basket, turned and ran off shouting, "Help, help, the cakes are going to eat me, the cakes are going to eat me!"

As soon as the bear was off and away, out of the basket popped Masha.

Oh, how happy Granny was to see her and how happy Masha was to see her granny! They hugged and kissed each other so many times that there were no kisses left till the next day.

"What a clever girl you are to trick that massive muscly bear," said Granny.

"Never mind that," said Masha. "Let's get these cakes inside us."

And that's what they did. Yum, yum and yum again!

THE GREAT GOLDEN BELLY-BUTTON

King Jabber sat watching the show.

The Ding-a-ling Brothers were singing their song, "If I Was A Pudding, I'd Ask You To Be The Custard".

Oh dear, it was the 39th time he'd heard it and he hadn't liked it the first time. Yawn, yawn, yawn.

Then Donk the jester came on and told jokes. They were all terrible – especially the long one about the pig that ate the King's underpants.

When Wizzo the wizard stood on the stage and said that he was going to take a rabbit and a donkey out of his hat, King Jabber couldn't take any more.

He stood up and said, "I can't stand any more of this rubbish. I want fun, I want laughter, I want ... I want ... egg on toast."

Everyone ran away and Bradstock, the King's servant, brought in the egg on toast. The toast was soggy. The egg was burnt. Or was it the other way round?

"I'm the king around here," said
Jabber. "I'm royal and you're loyal. I
sit about and do nothing all day, and
you're really glad you've got a king, even
if I cost bags and bags of money, and
then we're all terribly, terribly happy.
But what happens? I'm bored and the
Ding-a-ling Brothers are still singing
that stupid song about the pudding and
the custard. What am I going to do,
Bradstock?"

"First of all, sir, can I tell you that you have a little egg on your chin that perhaps you might want to wipe off? And then perhaps, sir, you might want to remember the Great Golden Belly-button you had made?"

"Yes, yes, yes, Bradstock. I do remember it. What of it?"

"Well, sir," said Bradstock, "you don't seem to have found much use for it yet."

"Use? Use? You don't use a Great Golden Belly-button. It just is. I had it made because it's a good sight more fun than listening to Wizzo, Donk and the Ding-a-lings."

"I understand, sir," said Bradstock, "but perhaps, sir, you might like to give it away as a sort of prize. The person who can make you laugh the most will win the Great Golden Belly-button."

"No, Bradstock, anyone can make me laugh. It's too easy. I've got a better idea. The person who tells the biggest lie will win the Great Golden Belly-button. How about that?"

"Excellent idea, sir!"

So the herald went out all around the country telling people: "Hear this! Hear this! Whoever is the biggest liar in all the land will win the Great Golden Belly-button from King Jabber himself."

It wasn't long before the palace was packed with people telling lies.

There was the woman who said she
had a horse that could say "hot dogs";
the man who said he had grass growing

in his armpits; the woman who said she
could swallow chairs, and so on and
so on.

Once again, King Jabber was getting bored.

"It's time we ended this stupid game of yours, Bradstock."

"Your stupid game, sir."

"Yours!"

"Yours!"

"Yours!"

Just then a voice piped up, "I'm here."

Bradstock and King Jabber looked round and there stood a small girl with a bowl in her hand.

"Who are you?" asked the King.

"Oh, come on," said the girl, whose name was Peggy. "You remember me, don't you? You owe me a hundred gold coins. I've come to collect them in my bowl here. It did have cornflakes in, but it's clean now."

"A hundred gold coins? A hundred gold coins?" said the King. "I've never seen you before in my life. I've never promised you any money and you're a liar to say I have."

"You promised. You did!"

"Did you hear that, Bradstock? Have you ever heard a liar like this little sprat? Get out of here, girl, before I set my dogs on you."

"Just hold it right there," said Peggy. "If you've never heard a liar like me before, then you must give me the Great Golden Belly-button."

"Ah. Er, well. Er, no ..." said the King. "Of course I didn't mean you were really a liar, I, er ..."

"Oh well, if I'm not a liar, then give me my hundred coins of gold," said Peggy.

There was silence. Bradstock waited for the order to set the dogs on her.

"Well, sock me sideways, the little sprat has done it!" said King Jabber. "Girl, the Great Gold Belly-button is yours. Give it to her, Bradstock."

Bradstock gave Peggy the Belly-button and she left the palace with it in her breakfast bowl.

"Stupid game you thought up there," said the King to Bradstock.

"Stupid game *you* thought up, sir," said Bradstock.

"No, *you* thought up."

"No, *you* thought up."

"*You* thought up."

"More egg on toast, sir?"

"I suppose so," said the King.

Our books are tested
for children and young people by
children and young people.

Thanks to everyone who consulted on
a manuscript for their time and effort in
helping us to make our books better
for our readers.

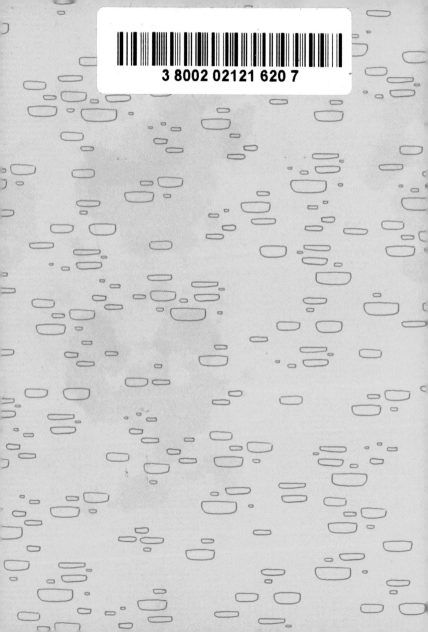